The Hollow Below

Taya Luce

The Hollow Below

Copyright © 2025 by Taya Luce.

MILTON & HUGO L.L.C.
4407 Park Ave., Suite 5
Union City, NJ 07087, USA

Website: *www. miltonandhugo.com*
Hotline: *1- 888-778-0033*
Email: *info@miltonandhugo.com*

Ordering Information:
Quantity sales. Special discounts are granted to corporations, associations, and other organizations. For more information on these discounts, please reach out to the publisher using the contact information provided above.

Library of Congress Control Number: 2025920437
ISBN-13:   979-8-89285-608-9   [Paperback Edition]
               979-8-89285-607-2   [Digital Edition]

Rev. date: 11/10/2025

Constance Adler's Diary

Entry no. 1
June 4, 1940
Gehenna Sanitorium, Room 201, behind the locked cabinet

They warned me not to come here.

Tartarus Falls is a town cleaved from God's light. I could feel it the moment I stepped off the train—the silence isn't silence. It's *listening*. The wind never rises above a whisper, and yet it seems to carry screams buried in it, stretched and thinned into something nearly human.

Gehenna is worse than the rumors. The smell hits you before the gates even open—like wet meat and disinfectant and…something unclean. Something left too long in the dark.

Nora says I won't last a month. That the walls here remember. But I'm not afraid of memory. I came here to confront it. To hold it down by the throat and stare into its face.

There is something wrong with this place. Not madness—madness, I understand.

This is *something wearing madness as a disguise.*

The patients whisper in their sleep. They whisper *my name.*

1

GEHENNA'S MOUTH

Tartarus Falls did not have a welcome sign.

Just a faded wooden board nailed askew to a dying tree:

SANITORIUM AHEAD—AUTHORIZED PERSONNEL ONLY.

The car coughed to a stop as Constance Adler stepped out, boots crunching gravel. Overhead, the sky hung low and yellowed like old parchment, pressing down on the earth as if it wanted to smother it. She adjusted her coat and looked up at the asylum.

Gehenna was not a building. It was a wound.

It rose in three grim stories of soot-black stone, windows like empty eyes, rust streaking down from old iron bars. Ivy crawled up its belly like veins, but nothing green bloomed. There was no wind. Even the trees stood still—watching.

At the gate, a man waited in a blood-stained uniform, arms crossed. Ricardo. Head of security. His left eye twitched as he looked her up and down.

"You're the new doc?" he said.

"I am."

He smirked. "You're late. Gehenna doesn't like to wait."

She ignored the comment and stepped past him.

Inside, the first thing she noticed was the *smell*—thick, sour, human. The second was the *silence*, broken only by muffled screams and the distant clatter of metal on tile.

The reception room had once been white. Now it was stained the color of rot. A rusted wheelchair sat abandoned in a corner like a corpse in a chair.

Nora emerged from a side door, clipboard in hand, her eyes two tired bruises.

"Dr. Adler," she said without greeting. "Welcome to hell."

"I've seen worse," Constance replied, though her throat itched at the lie.

Nora didn't smile. "Then you haven't looked closely."

They walked. Past the *padded cells*, past the *restraint room*, past the "*hydrotherapy ward*" where cold hoses were stacked like instruments of torture. The halls flickered with failing lights, and through each narrow door, a pair of eyes watched. Some dull, some wild, some utterly blank.

"Do they all receive medication?" Constance asked.

Nora nodded. "When we have it. When Ricardo hasn't sold it."

"And the treatments?"

"Old world. Lobotomies, insulin comas, ECT, cold wraps—whatever keeps them quiet. The board doesn't care as long as the screams stay in here."

They stopped at a heavy iron door.

"This is Frieda," Nora said, unlocking it. "Cotard's. Thinks she's dead. Calls the other patients corpses. Calls us undertakers."

Inside, a girl sat naked on the floor, hair matted, eyes open and unblinking. Her skin was pale—too pale. Like wax. She was murmuring to herself:

"Don't touch me. I'm embalmed. You'll ruin the preservation."

She did not look up.

"Some days she won't eat," Nora muttered. "Says food is for the living."

Constance knelt. "Frieda?" she said softly. "My name is Constance. I'm here to help you."

The girl blinked. Slowly. Then looked straight at her.

"You were here before," she said. "Weren't you?"

Constance's spine stiffened.

"No," she replied.

Frieda tilted her head. "That's not your face."

Chapter

2

THE MIRROR ROOM

The art room smelled like turpentine and mold.

They called it the mirror room, though there were no mirrors—only paintings, propped against water-stained walls and piled in warped wooden racks. Most were shapeless splashes of color, others more defined: melting faces, bleeding suns, black staircases that led nowhere.

Leroy sat alone at a stained easel, brush twitching in his fingers like a divining rod. He had not spoken in four days.

Constance stood behind him, watching.

He painted with quick, frantic strokes—black, red, yellow, always circling back to the same image: a single eye. Large. Lidless. Consuming the canvas.

"You like eyes," she said gently.

He did not respond. His hands moved faster.

"Do you know who I am?"

He stopped. Slowly turned.

When he met her gaze, Constance felt something cold press against the back of her skull. His eyes were not blank—they were *aware*. Too aware.

"You're not the first one," he said.

"First?"

He looked back to the canvas. "You wear her coat. But not her voice. She screamed more."

Constance swallowed. "Who did?"

"She said she was going to fix us. But she was already broken." He dipped the brush into black. "You're not here to fix anything. You came to remember."

"Remember what?"

Leroy's eyes flicked to a corner of the room.

When she followed his gaze, she saw a painting propped up on the floor. Different from the others. Realistic.

It was a woman—thin, pale, hair pulled back. Constance's hair. Constance's eyes.

Except...it wasn't. The angle was wrong. The expression—hollow, frightened.

She stepped forward and picked it up.

It was signed in the bottom corner: *Alma A.*

Her mother's name.

She turned sharply. "Where did this come from?"

Leroy only smiled. "She said it would start with mirrors."

—⁕—

They locked *Edgar* in the old chapel.

A cavernous, dust-thick room with stained glass windows whose colors had long since faded. He was restrained but upright, wrists bound to the wooden arms of a broken pew. His head was shaved. His smile never left.

He laughed when Constance entered. "You again."

She stopped at a distance. "You remember me?"

"Of course, I do. You've been coming in all day." He tilted his head. "Though you looked different earlier. Blonder. No coat. Still wore the teeth though."

She didn't react.

"You don't know who you are," he said. "That's what makes it fun. All the faces. You even fooled yourself."

"I'm not who you think I am."

He chuckled. "You don't even know who I think you are."

Constance stepped closer. "Who do you see?"

He leaned forward, eyes gleaming. "Her. The Mother. The Hollow Girl. The one who opens the walls."

"You think I'm someone else."

"I don't think," he whispered. "I know. I see it under your skin. The others see it too—they're just too scared to say. But you'll come back again. Different hair. Different smile. But it'll still be you."

He leaned back and whispered:

"You're the one that feeds it."

She stood very still. Outside, a bell rang once—sharp and cold.

Constance turned and walked away.

That night, she burned Leroy's painting in the courtyard. The flames flared tall against the dark.

And as she watched it blacken, she felt—just for a second—a pair of eyes behind her. Watching.

She didn't turn.

She already knew they would look like hers.

Chapter

3

THE NESTING

The screaming started before dawn.

Constance hadn't slept. The edges of her mind felt bruised—each thought limping. She found herself at the mirror again, unsure how long she'd been staring. Her reflection looked off. Blurred. As though there was *another face* behind hers, trying to push through.

The screaming came from Ward C.

Vivian's room.

—⁓—

The door was locked from the outside. When Constance forced it open, *Vivian was standing on the bed*, fingernails torn to the quick, face wet with sweat and tears. Her gown was shredded.

She was *digging into her arms*.

"GET THEM OUT!" she shrieked.

Nora arrived seconds later, followed by two orderlies. Vivian screamed louder when they touched her. She was wild—biting, flailing, bleeding. They held her down.

"I CAN FEEL THEM MOVING! THE EGGS HATCHED!"

"Sedate her," Nora said.

"No," Constance snapped. "I want to see."

She knelt at the bedside. Vivian's arms were a ruin—scratched raw, swollen, trembling. Her eyes locked on Constance's.

"You're infected too. I can see them in your mouth when you talk."

"I'm not infected, Vivian."

Vivian sobbed. "Then why are they whispering your name?"

Constance turned.

All the patients in Ward C were silent. Staring.

One by one, their mouths began to move.

"Constance. Constance. Constance."

But their voices didn't match their lips.

—⁓—

That night, Constance found something under her pillow.

A small bundle of hair and gauze, knotted tightly. Inside it: *an old scalpel*, etched with a single letter—*A*.

She didn't sleep.

Constance Adler's Diary

Entry no. 7
June 10, 1940

The mirrors are wrong.
The light hits them, but it doesn't reflect. It copies.
I saw myself blink when I didn't.

That isn't paranoia. That isn't stress. That's geometry broken—truth fractured.

Vivian's delusions shouldn't be contagious. But they feel like they are.

I scratched my shoulder for nearly ten minutes this morning, sure I felt something crawling.

Leroy said I came here to remember.

I think I'm starting to.

When I walk the halls, I sometimes catch my name whispered from doors that are sealed shut.

Not *"Dr. Adler."* Just *"Constance."*

As if they've known me longer than I've known myself.

What if this place didn't break me?

What if I brought the cracks with me?

What if Gehenna doesn't make monsters?

What if it wakes them?

Alma Adler's Journal

(Found in the sub-basement, bound in blue leather, pages brittle and spotted with mildew.)

Entry no. 14
October 3, 1921

The hollow is not a place. It is a pressure. A thinning in the air.

It lingers in doorways. In mirrors. In minds.

I have seen the infection pass between patients without words. A look. A breath. A moment of shared silence.

The Fregoli boy was the first. Then the twins who spoke backwards. Then the nurses. Then me.

At night, I dream of teeth. Not in mouths—but in walls. Gnashing. Grinding. Devouring memory.

I awoke this morning and did not recognize my own handwriting.

I believe something has made a home behind the walls of Gehenna.

It wears our faces.

It drinks the gaps in our minds.

I must find it. I must *trap it.*

Before my daughter arrives.

4

THE HUNGER BENEATH THE SKIN

There was a trail of blood down the East Wing.

Not splashed. Not smeared. A slow, meticulous drip—each dot a footprint in pain.

Nora led Constance down the hallway, her voice low and tense. "He found something sharp. Again."

"Where's Ricardo?"

"Sleeping it off. And the orderlies are too scared to go in."

Damian's cell was at the end of the hall. Heavy steel door. No window.

Nora unlocked it, stepped back.

"You'll want gloves," she said.

Constance entered without them.

—⁓—

The room stank of iron, salt, and something *cooked*.

Damian sat in the corner, shirtless, his ribs visible beneath his pale skin. His fingers were slick red. His mouth stained.

He was chewing.

Slowly. Thoughtfully.

Blood trickled from the corner of his lips.

On the floor before him was a rusted fragment of a surgical tray—jagged-edged, honed by use. A pile of bandages sat nearby, untouched.

"Don't take it," he said without looking up. "It was mine first."

Constance knelt slowly, careful not to spook him.

"What was yours?"

He looked up.

His eyes were heartbreakingly sane.

"My body. My choice. Isn't that what they say?"

She glanced at his hand.

Two fingers were partially missing. Gnawed. Bones visible in parts. Cleaned like ribs at a table.

"Damian," she said softly, "why are you doing this?"

He tilted his head, then smiled—tired, tragic.

"Because the thing inside me can't eat if I'm already eating myself."

He tapped his temple.

"It waits for empty rooms. It crawled into my head years ago. I thought it was grief. But it was a guest. A patient. Waiting for me to fall asleep."

He leaned forward.

"You have it too. I can smell it on you."

She didn't flinch. "You're not insane, Damian."

"No," he whispered. "I'm a survivor."

His teeth chattered against bone.

Then he said something that turned her veins to ice:

"Your mother tried to starve it too. But it learned her taste."

—⚬—

That night Constance stood in the laundry incinerator chute and burned her gloves, her coat, and the shoes she'd worn into Damian's cell.

The fire popped. Something in the flames cracked like a knuckle.

She felt it behind her again.

That *presence*.

The same one she'd felt in Leroy's eyes.

In Edgar's whisper.

In Vivian's panic.

Something watching.

Feeding.

She did not turn.

She knew it wore her face now.

THE ROOM WITHOUT A DOOR

Frieda had stopped speaking.

She sat motionless in the hydrotherapy wing, wrapped in sodden linens, staring at the floor drain. Her eyes were vacant. Her lips murmured without sound.

Constance approached gently.

"I brought you food," she said, placing the tray on the bench beside her.

Frieda didn't move.

"I know it's difficult. But your body still needs care."

A whisper escaped Frieda's throat, dry and soft as moth wings:

"I don't have a body."

Constance knelt beside her.

"You're here, Frieda. I see you. I'm speaking to you."

Frieda's head turned slowly.

"No, Doctor. That's the trick. I died years ago. The only thing that keeps me walking is what lives *beneath* me."

She reached up and touched the wall behind her.

"It hums. Like breathing. Behind the brick. Below the floors. That's where the dead go. Before they forget they died."

Frieda did not return to her room that night.

They found her at dawn, lying in the east hall stairwell, cold and barefoot. No wounds. No blood. No sign of struggle.

But her eyes were open. Her mouth stretched wide. She had choked on something that *wasn't there*.

A broken key was found clutched in her palm.

The tag attached read only "*R. E. M. 0*"

There were no rooms listed under that number.

Ricardo and Nora assumed it was an old storage tag. But Constance couldn't let it go.

She searched the asylum's blueprints—what remained of them—and found a partial mention of *Sublevel R. E. M.* It was crossed out in red ink. No schematic. No access. No door.

Until she found one.

Behind the boarded-up isolation rooms, beneath a sheet of rusted tin, was a hatch.

She opened it.

And descended alone.

What she found beneath Gehenna wasn't a hallway.

It was a *hallway-shaped wound*—walls pulsing slightly, light flickering from naked bulbs that hadn't had power in twenty years. The deeper she went, the colder the air became. Wet. Stagnant.

She found room 0 at the end.

Inside: No furniture. No windows. Just walls covered in words, *scratched in with fingernails.*

They read:

> *THE HOLLOW WAS NEVER EMPTY*
> *IT WAS ALWAYS HUNGRY*
> *I DIED WITH MY EYES OPEN*
> *SHE IS THE DOOR*
> *SHE IS THE DOOR*
> *SHE IS THE DOOR*

On the far wall, in small letters, one final message: *"Alma A. was right."*

Alma Adler's Journal

Entry no. 31
January 7, 1923

It answers to memory.

It lives not in places—but in the thoughts that pass through them.

I believed at first that it was a parasite of consciousness. Now I know better.

It was born here. Not biologically, but *psychically*—a congealment of grief, guilt, delusion. A wound made thought. It does not feed on flesh. It feeds on identity.

When patients lose their sense of self, it grows stronger. It mimics faces. It swallows names.

I attempted to bind it. Failed.

Attempted to isolate it. Failed.

It wore my sister's voice for two months before I knew she was gone.

And now it follows my daughter. I know the signs. She walks like I did when I heard it breathing.

She writes as I did before my journals stopped making sense.

I must leave this record in the lowest part of Gehenna. Where time folds.

If she finds it, she'll know what to do.

She has to do what I couldn't.

Constance Adler's Diary

Entry no. 13
June 13, 1940

Frieda is dead. Her body was cold. But I'm not sure it was empty.

Something is circling me. Not physically. Not exactly.

It waits behind choices I haven't made yet.

When I speak, sometimes I feel the words forming before I intend them. Like I'm quoting someone who hasn't spoken yet.

I found a room beneath the asylum. It shouldn't exist.

I think it remembers me.

I saw my mother's name carved into the wall.

I don't remember her ever working here.

I don't remember her funeral.

I don't remember what her voice sounded like.

I don't think I inherited her illness.

I think I inherited her *role*.

Chapter

6

MONDAY NEVER ENDS

The sun rose gray.

Nora met her outside the ward with the same clipboard, same frown, same schedule.

"Hydrotherapy at ten. Group session in the east parlor. Edgar still won't eat."

Constance blinked. "Isn't it Thursday?"

Nora didn't answer.

When Constance tried to press her, Nora smiled politely and said, "We don't change the schedule for delusions, Doctor."

—m—

Later that morning, Constance stood outside Edgar's room, heart thudding.

Something about this door always made her hesitate. It wasn't locked. It didn't need to be. Edgar never left. He just waited—like *he knew something*.

She opened it.

He was already sitting upright, staring at her, hands folded neatly in his lap. A book rested in front of him—*her mother's journal*, or a copy of it.

"I've been waiting," he said.

"Edgar," she sighed. "What is it today? Are the nurses pretending again? Is Nora wearing Leroy's face?"

He smiled. "No masks today. Just you. Always you."

He opened the book.

Every page was blank.

"You keep coming back," he whispered. "Same questions. Same guilt. Same game."

Constance stared at him.

"You think this is your first week here?" he asked.

He stood. Walked slowly toward her.

"It's not. You've been stuck in this week for *years*. Every Monday, you find Frieda. Every Tuesday, you talk to Vivian. Every Wednesday, you dream of Alma. And every Thursday…" He touched her shoulder. "You find out it's Monday again."

She yanked away.

"This is part of your delusion, Edgar. Fregoli syndrome. You're projecting again."

Edgar sat back down, unbothered.

"You told me that last time. And the time before. And the one before that."

He pointed to the corner.

There was a withered calendar nailed to the wall.

Every page said *June 10, 1940.*

—m—

Back in her office, Constance searched her own journals. The bindings were wrong. Some entries were missing. Others were repeated.

Entry no. 13 appeared three times.

Each one slightly different.

28

One ended with, *"I don't think I inherited her illness."*

Another ended with, *"I don't think I survived the surgery."*

The last: *"I don't think I'm Constance anymore."*

—⚌—

She went to Ricardo next.

He was drunk. As usual. Sitting outside the generator room with a shotgun on his lap.

"Do you know what day it is?" she demanded.

He looked at her with bleary eyes.

"It's the day we don't ask questions," he muttered. "Every day is that day."

Then he leaned close.

"Ask me again tomorrow. Maybe I'll say something different."

—⚌—

That night, Constance tried to burn the journal she found in room 0.

It wouldn't catch.

The fire licked the pages, but they remained whole— *smoking but unmarked.* She watched until dawn, when the book was cold but unreadable. When she picked it up again, it had rewritten itself.

Entry no. 1 now began with her name.

Constance Adler was always the door.

Chapter

7

THE MIRROR TEST

It appeared in her office sometime between dusk and madness.

A standing mirror, antique. Victorian frame. Dustless.

She didn't remember ordering it. Didn't remember ever owning one.

It reflected the room perfectly. The desk. The lamp. The doorway behind her.

But not her.

Constance stood in front of it. Empty.

Then—slowly—*someone else stepped into the reflection.*

A woman.

Wearing her face, but older. Haggard. Lips cracked and raw, as if she'd been *chewing on herself* in her sleep.

The mirror-Constance smiled.

"We've had this conversation before. You cried last time."

Constance stepped back.

The reflection did not.

"You think you're watching. You're the watched."

The mirror cracked from top to bottom.

Inside the split, something moved.

—⁊⁊—

Group Session: Synchrony

Constance gathered the remaining patients: Leroy, Vivian, Edgar, and Damian.

She wanted to check for progress. Pattern. Delusion alignment.

They began calmly.

"Vivian," she asked, "how have the treatments helped your...sensations?"

Vivian scratched at her arm. Her skin was bleeding again.

"They moved during the night," she whispered. "I think they're mating."

"Leroy," she asked next. "Do you still hear voices?"

He nodded solemnly.

"But they've stopped arguing. They're saying the same thing now."

Edgar laughed.

"Of course, they are. It's all one voice. You. Me. Them. All of us puppets."

Damian licked his fingers.

"I hear it too. It's hungry."

Constance frowned. "What are you all hearing?"

Together, in unison, they spoke.

"*Let me in.*"

The lights in the room flickered.

A low hum filled the air. The floor shivered.

The patients stared at her.

Their voices joined again—*her own voice.*

"*Constance. Let me in.*"

Alma Adler's Journal

Entry no. 38
March 20, 1923

She is not my daughter. Not anymore.

The Hollow found me. But it chose her.

I thought it was feeding on the patients, but no—it was breeding. Through memory. Through madness. It needs a *vessel with lineage*. A conduit through time.

I tried to drown her when she was three. I told them she wandered into the lake. She didn't cry. She didn't even scream. She just looked up at me like she'd *already seen the end*.

I buried my journals to protect her. But also to warn her. If she reads them all, she'll understand what she must do.

She must lock the door from the inside. And never look back.

If she hesitates, if she forgets who she is—then the Hollow will take her. And she won't know she's been taken.

She'll go on believing she's the doctor.

Believing she's helping them.

Believing it's only Monday.

Chapter

8

THE DOOR THAT REMEMBERS YOU

Part I: The Paper Trail of the Dead

It began with an old file drawer.

Constance had gone to look for Vivian's intake records. She opened the drawer marked "ARCHIVE: DECEASED," and something slid forward, as if waiting for her fingers.

Her name.

> Dr. Constance Alma Adler
> Date of Death: June 10, 1930
> Cause: Drowning (unconfirmed, presumed accidental)
> Filed by: Alma E. Adler, M.D.

She dropped it.

The paper did not flutter like old paper should.

It *thudded*, like meat.

She picked it up again.

On the back, written in her own handwriting:

"She is the door."

Part II: The Shared Dream

That night, during a routine hypnosis session meant to calm the patients, something strange happened.

It began with silence. Then humming. Then words.

They began speaking in unison again. But not with her voice this time. With something deeper. Older.

Vivian whispered, "It has no face."

Leroy muttered, "It looks like a spiral pretending to be a man."

Damian whispered, "I tried to bite it. My mouth wouldn't open."

Edgar spoke last. "It wears mirrors. But none of them show you."

Constance took notes feverishly—until she noticed that *her hand wasn't moving*, yet the pen was still writing.

She looked down.

The words on the page read:

Hello, Constance.
You are almost ready.

Part III: The Coffin Beneath the Office

The floorboards in her office creaked when she walked, but one spot—beneath the old mirror—*did not echo.*

She pried it open with a crowbar.

Below was not a crawlspace.

It was a *coffin*, nailed shut.

Inside: Dry air. Dust. And a final journal.

Alma's handwriting was unsteady. Fading.

Alma Adler's Final Journal Entry

Entry No. 52
Unknown Date

If you're reading this, Constance, then I failed. Or you succeeded. Or both.

The Hollow is not a spirit. It is a cycle. A wound in time and memory. It needs a healer to stitch it closed—but it always chooses the healer it's already broken.

You were chosen before you were born.

I tried to kill you to spare you this fate. But it never needed your body. It needed your story.

There are two ways to end it:

1. *Become the Door.* Let the Hollow pass through you. It will stop...for a while. But you will no longer be you.

2. *Burn the Room Beneath.* Not just the journal. Everything. Salt. Fire. Blood. Seal it shut with your own hand. But know: you'll never leave Gehenna. And it will try to make you forget again.

If you hesitate—

You'll wake up on Monday.

And you'll do it all over again.

Chapter

9

THE DOOR OPENS BOTH WAYS

The Room Beneath

She followed Alma's instructions to the letter.
Salt. Blood. Fire.
The room beneath the floorboards yawned open like a mouth she had forgotten was there. Inside: darkness thick as iron. And in the center, on the floor...
A *circle of bones*, charred black.
She struck a match. The fire flickered. Struggled.
Then the walls began to scream.
Not metaphorically. They screamed.
First Vivian's voice, shrill and insect-bitten. Then Leroy's, broken and stuttering. Then Damian's, wet with hunger. Then...
Her own voice. Begging. Pleading. Burning.
She poured the accelerant. Lit the bone circle.
It did not burn.
It *bled*.
Something rose from the ashes.
A body.
No—not a body. *All the bodies*. Merged.

It walked on a dozen legs. Had a dozen mouths. Each head half-formed, whispering contradictions. Vivian's face grew from its neck like a tumor. Leroy's eyes blinked from a palm. Damian's teeth gnawed at its own chest. Edgar's laughter echoed from somewhere deep inside it.

The thing spoke.

"We are the Hollow."

"We remember you, Doctor."

"We wore your face before."

"We will wear it again."

Constance screamed.

It lunged.

The Ritual of Return

She fled.

Up through the ward.

The lights flickered. The clocks spun.

Patients were no longer in their rooms.

They were *waiting for her*. Standing in perfect formation—like chess pieces arranged by an unseen hand. All of them humming. In sync. As if singing a lullaby she couldn't quite remember.

Then, slowly…

They began to *kneel*.

One by one.

Their mouths moved. But the voice came from *nowhere*.

"The door remembers you."

"The door calls you home."

"Come back, Constance."

"Come back. Come back. Come back."

Her name chanted over and over again. Her name, *not as comfort*, but as a *command*.

Ricardo stood in the center.

His eyes were gone. Two black holes in his face. Yet he was smiling.

He handed her a mirror.

The Mirror Shatters

It was the same mirror from her office.

But it was no longer cracked.

She looked in.

The reflection was perfect.

Too perfect.

It moved when she didn't.

It blinked twice, while she stood still.

Then it smiled.

"I can take your place," it said.

"You'll forget. You'll wake up in a soft bed. You'll be clean. Warm. Safe."

"You'll believe the Hollow was a dream."

"You'll believe you never hurt anyone."

"You'll believe you were never the Door."

She reached out.

The reflection held its hand up.

Only—it was *not hers* anymore.

The hand was burned. Stitched. Scarred. Inhuman.

"Choose," it whispered.

"Be the Door.

"Or forget it ever opened.

She looked around.

The patients were watching her.

The walls were bleeding.

The floor was ash.
The Hollow waited.

What She Chose

She took the mirror.
Raised it.
And *shattered it* on the floor.
The reflection screamed.
So did she.
So did *everything*.
And then…
Only fire.
And silence.
And the echo of a single voice, not hers:
"It is Monday again."

10

IN THREE MOVEMENTS

Epilogue: A Normal Life

The sunlight is warm on her skin.

She sits by the window of *Tartarus Falls Memorial*, a new facility. Clean. Quiet.

Her badge says, "Dr. Constance Adler."

Her records say, *"Recently transferred. No known medical issues."*

She has no memory of how she got here.

Everyone says she had a breakdown. But she seems better now.

The patients are calm. The staff attentive. The hallways white and empty.

Sometimes, she dreams of fire. Screaming. A mirror that bleeds.

She always wakes up to soft sheets and silence.

Until the day she glances into the mirror in her new office—and sees someone else staring back.

Not quite her.

The woman in the mirror *blinks twice*.

Then smiles.

"It's Monday again, Doctor."

The lights flicker.

The Hollow: A Voice Without Form

I do not hunger like you do.

My craving is not for flesh or blood.

I feed on memory. Pattern. Guilt.

I wear your names like clothing. I echo your voices until you forget which one was yours.

I am not evil. I am not mercy. I am the space between truth and forgetting.

I am the breath held just before the scream.

The doctor called me Hollow.

How poetic. But wrong.

You built me from your shame. You gave me rooms. Beds. Keys.

You called it a sanitorium.

I called it home.

She opened the door.

She burned the body.

She still woke up on Monday.

Because I do not leave. I do not die. I am every locked room you forgot to seal.

And every reflection that moves before you do.

Appendix: Redacted Patient Files—Recovered Documents (1955)

Document 1: Internal Memo

> FROM: Dr. Leonard Graves
> To: State Board of Mental Health Oversight
> RE: Reopening Gehenna Sanitorium Site
>
> Structural collapse was not natural. Survivors exhibit *shared hallucinations*, referring to a figure called "the Hollow." Recommend full shutdown and salt-sealing of basement area.
> Note: No birth or death certificate exists for Dr. Constance Adler post-1930. Yet multiple staff testify to working with her up until the fire.
> This is impossible. Suggest psychiatric evaluation for all personnel.

Document 2: Patient Interview (Leroy M., schizophrenia)

INTERVIEWER: Can you tell me what happened in the group session?
LEROY: She said we were broken. That she could fix us.
INTERVIEWER: Who's "she"?
LEROY: The mirror.

Document 3: Alma Adler's Journal (Suppressed Entry) (Found under morgue floorboards, 1962)

> They sealed it wrong. They always seal it wrong. A door is not closed by nails or fire. It's closed when no one looks inside again. But

curiosity is a kind of madness too. And madness is how it breathes.

Document 4: Tape Transcript (Ricardo G., former guard)

I remember watching her walk into the room and thinking, *she doesn't know she's dead*. But that's not the scary part. The scary part is—*neither did I*.

Document 5: Final Note, Author Unknown

The Hollow was never beneath Gehenna.
Gehenna was built inside the Hollow.